Monday	Tuesday	Wednesday	Thursday	Friday	Saturday
	1	2	3	4	5
8	9	10	11	12	
Home!	Plumber to fix tub / Call Babysitter	Pick up Dry Cleaning		Theater 8:00	Library
Maddie's Party	15	16	17		
	11:00 Felix - Dentist Dr. Scott	11:30 Lunch with Pau	Flying Lesson / Pick up Corey, Clark		Uncle Will Arrives!
22	23	24	25	26	
	Lunch with Charlie + Sam / 6:30 Preschool Meeting	Manicure / Felix - Playdate. Cleo's house.	Elli's Birthday.	IAN Here. / 7:00 PM Marshmellow Roast	
30	31			Bread Milk. eggs Canned pinapple carrots	
Dinner w/ Grammy	Buy hotdogs / 12:00 Barbeque st. George's.				

Castle Dry Cleaning
1200 Kings Road
Your cleaning will be ready:
Wed. 1-9 ✗
011098

No Hugs Till Saturday

JULIE DOWNING

Clarion Books • New York

Clarion Books, a Houghton Mifflin Company imprint, 215 Park Avenue South, New York, NY 10003

Copyright © 2008 by Julie Downing

The illustrations were executed in watercolor and colored pencil. The text was set in 16-point Melior.

For information about permission to reproduce selections from this book, write to Permissions, Houghton Mifflin Company, 215 Park Avenue South, New York, NY 10003.

www.clarionbooks.com

Printed in Singapore

Library of Congress Cataloging-in-Publication Data
Downing, Julie. No hugs till Saturday / by Julie Downing.
p. cm. Summary: When Felix declares that there will be no hugs, snuggles, or super squeezes for a whole week, both he and his mama have a hard time. ISBN-13: 978-0-618-91078-6 [1. Hugging—Fiction. 2. Mothers and sons—Fiction. 3. Week—Fiction.] I. Title. PZ7.D75928No 2008 [E]—dc22 2007010030

TWP 10 9 8 7 6 5 4 3 2 1

Hugs to my posse,
Betsy, Judy, and Katherine,
and a super-special gigantic
hug to my son, Will

On Sunday morning, Felix leaped out of bed. "Time for your Good Morning hug," he sang. "Do you want a soft snuggle, a super squeeze, or a monster mash?"

Mama smiled. "A super squeeze will start my day out just right."

Felix gave her an extra-special one.

After breakfast, Felix put on his cape and tossed his favorite ball. *Thwack!* A perfect Super Dragon throw.

"Felix!" Mama called. "Remember the rule. No playing ball in the house."

Tomorrow Shelf

8

Mama picked up the ball and put it away. "Now, you need some quiet time. No more ball until tomorrow."

When quiet time was over, Mama was ready with a hug.
"No more hugs!" Felix announced. "No hugs till Saturday."
"No snuggles?" asked Mama.
Felix shook his head.
"How about a super squeeze or a monster mash?"
Felix shook his head. "No hugs at all."

"Oh, dear," Mama said. "That's too bad."

"Super Dragons don't give
hugs!" Felix jumped and made
a perfect landing.

"Super Dragons don't *need* hugs!"
He jumped again.

But this time he didn't make such
a good landing.

Mama came
running. "A hug
will make it better."

"No!" Felix said.
"No hugs till Saturday."

"Not even a cuddle?"
Mama asked.

"No hugs at all," said Felix.

14

"Such a long time," Mama said with a sigh.

Felix went to the kitchen for a drink.

"Mama," asked Felix. "Is it Saturday yet?"

"No, sweetie. Today is Sunday. There's a whole week until Saturday."

Felix thought for a while. "What day comes before Saturday?"

Mama showed him.

"Tomorrow is Monday. Then come Tuesday, Wednesday, Thursday, and Friday."

"Actually, I meant no hugs until Friday," said Felix.

Mama frowned. "But that's still five days away."

Felix went into his room and stacked his blocks,
one on top of the other.

Mama clapped when she saw the tower. "It's as tall as you. You deserve a big hug."

Felix opened his arms—but then he remembered. "I can't hug you till Friday."

"Oh, dear," said Mama. "I forgot, too."

Felix rode his bike around the house. As he passed Mama, he asked, "What day comes before Friday?"

"Thursday," said Mama.

"Is that still a long time?"

She nodded. "Monday, Tuesday, and Wednesday all come before Thursday."

"Well, I really meant no hugs till Thursday,"
Felix said. "No hugs at all."

By lunchtime, Felix could tell
Mama was missing his hugs.

"Mama," Felix called. "There are no hugs till Tuesday. No hugs at all!"

"What happened to Wednesday?" asked Mama.

"I'm afraid you'll drown before then from so many slobbery baby hugs."

After lunch, Felix and Mama
settled down for a movie.

Felix jumped
at a scary bit.

"That wasn't a hug!" he said. "I just wanted more popcorn. There are still no hugs till Tuesday."

Mama passed Felix the bowl of popcorn. "I don't know if I can wait two more days," she said.

"Two days?" Felix gulped. "I really meant no hugs till Monday. No hugs at all."

"Monday is tomorrow," Mama said. "I hope I can last that long."

Felix could hardly wait until tomorrow.

At bedtime, Felix chose a book to read. He thought about his bedtime hug.

"Mama, is it tomorrow yet?" he asked.

Mama shook her head. "Not until you wake up."

Suddenly, Felix knew it was going to be a long night.

"Mama, I think it's not good for me to go so long without a hug," he said.

"It's not good for me, either," agreed Mama.

Felix slid next to Mama. "What kind of bedtime hug do you want?" he asked. "A soft snuggle, a super squeeze, or a monster mash?"

Mama smiled. "I think I need a super, special, gigantic monster mash!"

So Felix gave her one for Sunday. And then he gave her six more.

One for Monday.

One for Tuesday.

One for Wednesday.

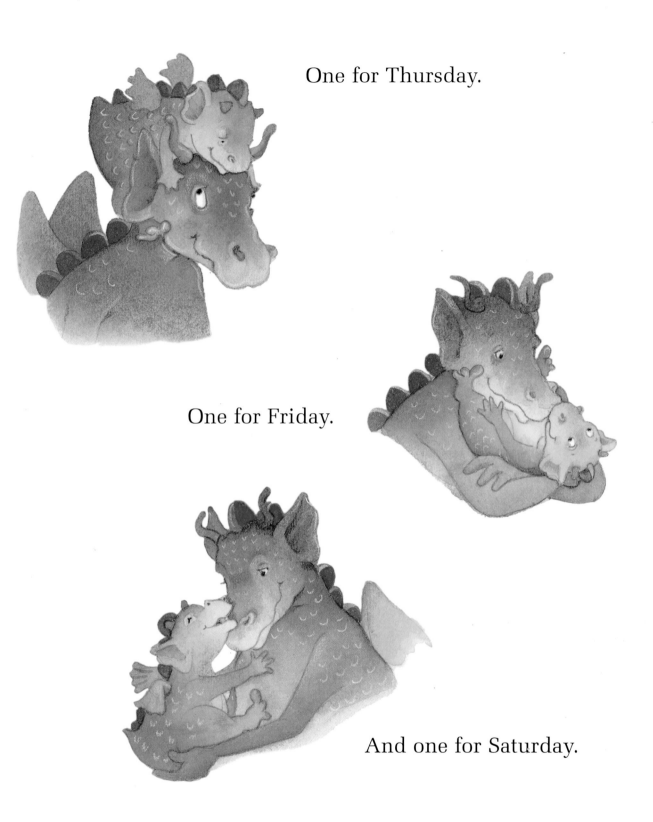

One for Thursday.

One for Friday.

And one for Saturday.

A whole week of hugs for Mama.